5

Rose's Unexpected Tragedy

Phyllis A. Collmann

ISBN: 978-1-57579-386-3

Library of Congress Control Number: 2008935128

For additional copies of this or other
books written by Phyllis Collmann:
pac51@hickorytech.net
712-552-2375
www.collmannwarehouse.com

Printed in the United States of America

PINE HILL PRESS
4000 West 57th Street
Sioux Falls, SD 57106

⁓ Dedication ⁓

This is the fifth book in the series of Rose Donlin.
The book is dedicated to my husband, Colin.

To the wonderful people I have meant on this journey
since I started writing. For the wonderful words... "I
love your books." I am so grateful.

To my children,
Cynthia, Kimberly, Ronald and Melonie.

To all of my grandchildren and
great-grandchildren... I love you all.

∽ About the Author ∾

Phyllis A. Collmann is a retired nurse. She has lived on the same farm for 45 years with her husband of 56 years. This is the fifth book about Rose Donlin. It is a sequel to her first, second, third and fourth pioneer book. The first book is called *Rose's Betrayal and Survival*. The second book is called *Rose's Triumphant Return* and the third is called *Rose's Heart's Decision*. The fourth book is called *Rose's Dream Fulfilled*.

Published books:
  Rose's Betrayal and Survival
  Rose's Triumphant Return
  Rose's Heart's Decision
  Rose's Dream Fulfilled
  Rose's Unexpected Tragedy

  Kim's Unplanned Sega
  Mother's Innocence Proven
  Christmas At Our House

A Very Special Thank You

Julie Ann Madden   Diane Ten Napel
Norma Kay Wendt   Kimberly Ann Bonnett

The cover is very unique to me.

The twins are Blake P. and Brenna O.,
children of Brad and Megan Dirksen.

The baby is Morrison Rose Luban,
daughter of Dr. Jeff and Melonie
Collmann Luban.

⌒ Chapter 1 ⌒

Rose couldn't move. Henry's arms were wrapped tightly around her making it impossible for her to move. She could feel the strength of his muscular arms. He was waiting for an answer. He had just asked her to marry him this very day. This was the third time he had asked her and he wanted an answer this very minute.

Rose's smile indicated how very happy she was feeling. She opened her mouth but hesitated before saying, "Nothing would make me happier."

"Is that a yes?" Henry said without loosening his hold on her.

"Yes is my answer," then added. "Henry, I will marry you in 30 days, right here on this very spot." To Rose, Henry would be the kind of husband every girl dreams of.

"I will ask the renters to build our cabin," she said. "We'll spend our first night in our new cabin that has many rooms."

Henry looked deep into Rose's eyes and with his usual smile said, "Rose Donlin, you have a deal."

The sky was clear with no clouds, making the sky a true blue color. The prairie grass moved ever so slowly in a gentle breeze. Trees surrounded them, making the site for the new cabin very private and a very peaceful place to raise a large family with Henry.

Rose had found this quiet, perfect spot after she had been swimming in Joseph's creek. She had needed a place she could go to be alone. Now it would be turned into her new homestead where she could live the rest of her life with the man she loved.

Henry released his tight hold on her but she did not move. They stood with their arms around each other and each loves the warmth of the other's body.

❧ *Chapter 2* ❧

Henry had been asked by Rose to begin drilling for oil on her land. This was a large project and Rose knew Henry Helgens was the only man she could trust to complete this huge undertaking. She believed him to be strong. She believed him to do everything she asked of him.

The first site of oil Rose found was underground in the food cellar. Rose had only been at Joseph's cabin a very short time when she went down into the cave. She had wanted to find some food to prepare for them to eat as there had not been any in the cabin. She had stepped down from the last step and she found she was standing in some black sticky liquid. The next time she saw the same kind of black, wet, thick shiny liquid was out in a field. She was hunting for a rabbit to put in a trap to catch a mountain lion.

Henry knew this would not be considered a wild cat drilling because the oil was already there. He would not have to search.

Henry helped Rose up into the buggy and sat close beside her. He drove her to the hospital and explained to her, "I'm going into Oklahoma City to register for a license to build several oil drilling pumps."

⌒ Chapter 3 ⌒

Henry located the office. The name on the door read. "OIL AND DRILLER'S LICENSE-----DRILL PUMPS"

The man sitting behind the desk was dressed in a black suit. He had a full beard, making it impossible to really tell what he looked like. He was wearing a pair of silver rimmed glasses that sat on the end of his slightly thin, over sized nose. A chain was connected to one side, hanging hooked to his suit jacket. His hair had streaks of grey.

He opened the door after hearing Henry knock. His voice was firm, and there was no warm greeting. His forehead was wrinkled with a frown.

Wiley Rineheart was a lonely man who had never married and was still living with his mother. Henry put his hand out in a gesture to shake his hand. Wiley Rineheart stood looking and studying Henry closely.

"Come in," his voice sounded as if he wanted Henry to know he was in charge and whatever Henry wanted, he would have the last word. He looked over the top of his glasses at Henry, his eyes squinted almost closed.

"What do you want?" Wiley Rineheart said.

Henry took a deep breath and then opened his mouth to answer but before he could say a word Wiley Rineheart said, "What did you say your name was?"

Henry said, "My name is Henry Helgens. I want to drill for oil on Rose Donlin's land." Henry was trying not to show how angry he was suddenly feeling.

"Rose Donlin. Who is Rose Donlin?" Rineheart said with a nasty bitterness in his voice.

"Are you talking about Joseph Higgins' land?" His voice seemed to sound louder and more inquisitive.

"Joseph Higgins left all of his land to Rose Donlin. She would like to start drilling for oil immediately. I'd like to set up at least 3 drills this month and 3 more next month."

"Just a minute Mr. Helgens, first we have to have proof that Joseph Higgins' land is in Rose Donlin's name."

Suddenly Henry was aware something was going on with this little man. Wiley Rineheart was carrying a grudge. Henry knew he had to get proof before Mr. Rineheart would go any further with the license and oil drills.

Henry was sure he was going to see this man turn into a hawk and fly right into his face. Rineheart's fingernails would be his claws and dig out Henry's eyes. Henry tried to clear this thought from his mind.

Something had happened in the past that Henry did not know about, and he was sure Rose did not know or she would have told him about it.

Henry blurted out, "Perhaps John Fitzpatrick should be at this meeting"

Rineheart, again squinted his eyes and drew in a deep breath then said loudly in an ugly tone, "That land should have been mine."

Henry jumped to his feet. He was on the way out of the door and heading straight for the bank and John Fitzpatrick. Henry's black Stetson just cleared the door frame as he entered the bank. The chain from his belt that connected to his brown leather money holder made a jingling noise alerting John Fitzpatrick someone had entered the bank.

∽ Chapter 4 ∽

The two men's eyes met and John recognized the man whom Rose Donlin had chosen over him. John had never felt a loss or a set back until Henry Helgens came into Rose's life. John was tempted to let the woman who worked in the bank wait on Henry, but he knew at some point in time he would have to deal with Henry Helgens.

John had only resentment and envy for Henry Helgens.

Henry, at this particular time, felt the need to straighten up this dispute over Rose's land.

"My name is Henry Helgens."

Henry did not let John Fitzpatrick reach out to shake hands of say anything.

Henry spoke immediately saying, "I just came from Wiley Rineheart's office, and he claims the land of Rose Donlin should be his. I would like to clear this all up."

John's reaction was slow. He finally said, "Please step into my office."

"Wiley Rineheart came to this area saying, he was related to Joseph Higgins' mother. Joseph denied there was any relationship between his mother and Wiley Rineheart. He refused to have anything to do with him. So, Wiley thought if he started an oil drilling company, Joseph would eventually come into his office."

"Wiley had heard there were many pools of oil bubbling up onto the surface of Joseph's land. Joseph refused to drill the oil on his land but he did tell Rose to drill when she was ready."

John's voice was shaky when he first began to talk; now he sounded sure and confident.

Henry opened his mouth, ready to speak but before he could. John said, "I, I can help, if you would like. I could work with Wiley, to order the drilling machines."

Henry took in a deep breath, pushed his chair back and stood up. He took a step toward the door then turned, looking directly into John's eyes, and said with an angry sound in his voice, "I do not need help with Wiley Rineheart now that I know the land is in Rose Donlin's name."

Henry opened John's office door and walked out of the bank. He headed directly across the street to Rineheart's oil drilling office. His steps were long and fast.

Mr. Rineheart jumped up from behind his desk, yelling, "You did not knock."

"That's right," Henry yelled back. "I'm here to order three drilling machines. I want them on Rose Donlin's land in one week. Don't make me come back in here with Sheriff Les." Henry left as angry as he had entered the office.

⌒ Chapter 5 ⌒

The ride home was a time for Henry to calm down and think about the cabin being built for Rose and him. He would make sure the wedding night in the cabin would be prefect.

The wedding date was only two weeks away. Rose's renters were all working many hours each day. The cabin stood on a plot of ground surrounded by tall trees that overlooked a thousand acres of green grass. The trees were home to many kinds of birds. Rabbits ran free in the tall grass.

The cabin had many rooms with a large porch that wrapped completely around the cabin. He was determined to make Rose happy. He dreamed of sitting side-by-side on the porch watching the sun go down, watching the stars come into view, to make the evenings very romantic.

Henry stopped at the cabin and worked with the men until darkness completed another day of work. Toby was always in charge when Henry was not there.

Henry and Toby had becomes friends after many difficult situations. Toby was or had thought he was in love with Rose. He had never met anyone like her. He was infatuated with her kindness, her strength and most of all her beauty.

Henry fell in love with Rose on the month-long trip they took together from outside of St. Louis, Missouri, into Oklahoma City. Rose found Henry to be strong, kind and gentle. He took control of her life, keeping her safe while traveling with her across Missouri. Taking Rose safely back to Oklahoma City was his only concern. He had delivered her just like he promised he would. He was very dependable.

The meeting between Toby and Mary started out being difficult for each one. After getting acquainted with Mary and her daughters, Toby spent time with Elizabeth and Sarah. He found himself liking them and wanting to protect them. He spent time with Mary before and after Hank, her son, was born. It didn't take Toby long to realize his mind was always drifting off and wondering what Mary was doing. He wanted to help take care of Elizabeth and Sarah and Hank and most of all he wanted Mary for his own. When Toby realized that, Henry and Toby became good friends.

Chapter 6

The cabin was nearly completed. The last few boards were ready to go on. The wedding would take place right in front of the cabin among the tall trees where the wind blew against the leaves, gently making a whispering sound.

The honeymoon would be spent right in the cabin after the guests had left for their own homes. Henry wanted to have all of the oil drills in place and working. The oil was bubbling up on more land.

Chapter 7

The following morning the big oil drills came in wagons pulled by six large horses. Toby, Rufus George and Henry worked long days getting the drills down the holes. This was not a wildcat well. They were not searching into the ground not knowing for sure if oil was there, the oil was already appearing on top of the ground. The work was hard and dirty, making everyone look black by the day's end.

The big rigs were welded in Oklahoma City. Then taken apart and loaded in the wagons. After they arrived at the oil spills, again, the parts were put together. Ropes were used to pull each section on top of the next. Then each section was bolted together.

Three of the large oil drills were in place and the plan was to turn each big motor on. The first motor started, and the three men stood clear and waited. No one spoke.

The noise from below was deafening. Rumbling, gurgling and then the explosive force the oil blew up, gushing high into the air. The oil covering the men did not stop the joy each one was feeling. A roar of laughter showed how happy they felt seeing the oil. As they looked at each other, another roar went up as they all looked like Rufus George—black like him.

The black shinny oil would be capped and pumped into barrels.

Rose was right; oil was a big job to get to market. She was also right to give the job to Henry.

❧ Chapter 8 ❧

The sun could not have been any brighter. It woke Rose shinning in on her face.

Her first thought was this was the day she had waited for since she realized she had fallen in love with Henry Helgens. She felt excited. She felt she had made the right decision to marry Henry Helgens this very day.

Rose had stayed the night at the hospital in Mary's room. Mary, Elizabeth, Sarah and Hank stayed with Maude.

The cabin was where all of Henry's family was staying. His family consisted of eighteen siblings, his mother and father.

No one would be left out. Their lives had touched many people. They wanted to share this day with family and friends. Rose was well known and now Henry.

Even the birds started the day singing. In every tree different birds sang as if they all had been invited.

The rain the morning before left a spring smell in the air. The grass around the cabin had a dark green color.

Everything looked prefect. The cook at the hospital prepared the food for all of the invited guests, and the people who dropped in uninvited. All were welcome.

All of the renters came with their children. The front yard of the cabin was filled with excitement, laughter and joy. The little children were running, jumping and giggling.

The minister from Oklahoma City came out from town to perform the ceremony. He stepped out from the cabin door. A giant cheer went up from the people.

From around behind the cabin one of Henry's brothers walked up first to stand in front of the minister. Thomas, Henry's youngest brother came next. He wore a black suit that matched his two brothers.

Henry came next. He had a new black suit with a white shirt that had ruffles on the collar and the cuffs. He wore cowboy boots trimmed in black. The black Stetson hat covered his dark curly hair. He looked like a statue of greatness.

The smile on his face showed the happiness he felt throughout his body. Everyone there knew Henry had chosen Rose Donlin to spend the rest of his life with. He stood waiting for the love of his life to come out of the cabin door.

The door of the cabin opened slowly, Mary stepped out first. Toby stood off to the side. As he watched her walk down the steps carefully. He knew at that precise minute he was going to ask her to marry him.

Everyone's eyes again returned to the cabin door.

Thomas took a couple of steps and headed toward the stair steps. He walked up the stairs, across the porch, and opened the door.

Rose's Unexpected Tragedy

Rose stood in the doorway. The hush over the witnesses and the drawing in of the crowd's breath was an outpouring of love. Her beauty was seen by everyone.

The beautiful white dress she wore was made by Mary and her. A lovely silk pink ribbon hung down from her hair. Her boots were white. They laced up beyond her ankles.

Rose paused on the porch and smiled back at Henry.

Then in an instant, her eyes went to the crowd as an elderly man stepped out and walked toward her. The surprise was overwhelming for Rose. Henry had secretly sent for her father, Louis Donlin from St. Louis, Missouri.

Rose had forgiven her father. Over five years before, Louis had abruptly sent his daughter away from the only home she had ever known. He had completely changed her life. It was more difficult than anyone could ever imagine.

The man her father sent her too, was Joseph Higgins. He was an elderly sick man. The hurt had all disappeared over the years because Rose had accepted her new life. She ended up loving Joseph with respect and companionship.

Louis walked up to her and held out his arm. Rose took his arm and could not have been happier. They looked at each other with tears in their eyes. She had totally forgiven him.

∽ Chapter 9 ∽

Louis stepped up beside Henry and placed Rose's hand in his.

The silence from the visitors indicated no wanted to miss a word. The ceremony was short.

Henry and Rose looked into each other's eyes and swore to dedicate their entire life to each other. And always be ready to help the other if danger was close. The pledges to each other were honest and sincere.

When Henry kissed his new beautiful wife, he took her face gently in his hands and placed his lips on hers. No one but Henry and Rose mattered at that moment. Everyone there witnessed the kiss that prepared them for a life time together.

The happiness radiated to each one there. The party lasted late into the night before people left for their homes. The family would use the cabin one more night. Henry's brothers stayed in the new bunkhouse.

☙ Chapter 10 ❧

Henry had planned this wonderful night very carefully. First, he had found the area. The blankets were laid on the ground. He had placed lanterns around the blankets. The new blankets, he laid carefully folded to cover them for the night.

The night sky was filled with a million stars. The full moon was of a brilliant light and shown directly over them. They talked most of the night about the love they felt for each other. The promise they made to each other solemnly would be God first, then to hold the other above anyone, or anything else.

The long days planning the wedding, getting the family to the wedding caught up with them both and now their bodies relaxed and sleep was welcome. The morning was spent asleep on the blankets.

The following afternoon Henry and Rose returned to their new home. Everyone had gone.

Henry opened the door and then gently picked up his new bride. He stepped across the threshold and with his foot kicked the door closed. He carried Rose down the hall to there own private room. He kicked the door shut.

Henry and Rose became one.

ꝏ *Chapter 11* ꙅ

The oil well pumped day and night. The first three drills were working non-stop.

The barrels full of crude oil were put in a big old wagon. The wagon rumbled down the trail and was taken into Oklahoma City and to the railroad station. The barrels rode in the boxcars to the refinery.

Henry rode into town stopping outside of the drilling office for the second time. He knocked loudly on the door. He immediately recognized the voice coming from inside the office stating "come in."

Henry walked in feeling mentally alert, ready for another conflict. His eyes had a steely look. His body was taut and straight. He did not remove his black Stetson hat. As he stepped through the door, his hand made a fist.

Nothing had changed. Wiley Rineheart was sitting behind his desk in a ridged position. He looked up at Henry. His face showed anger and hostility. Henry was sure Mr. Rineheart recognized him as he came through the door. He also quickly grabbed the "Jack Daniels" bottle and set it down under his desk.

"I need 3 more oil drills and I need them as soon as I can get them." Henry said firmly.

"You can have them when I say you can." Wiley said abruptly while turning his chair so his back was to Henry. Then added. "Why do you need them, in such a hurry?"

Henry did not answer. He did not think it was any of Rineheart's business. He turned and walked out of the office feeling Mr. Rineheart was no longer a problem. He would never feel fear or uncertainty coming here again.

☙ Chapter 12 ❧

Rose was aware of the change in her body. She welcomed the happiness she felt within. She had a warm feeling. Henry's love was growing in her body.

She had frequently thought about the way the young Indian girl had looked after her baby had been born. Her cheeks were a light shade of pink. She had looked at her young Indian husband with love on her face.

Rose remembered the reaction from Mary when she placed Hank in her arms and the loving look on her face. Mary held him securely against her chest.

Now she was looking forward and anticipating the birth of her own baby. Telling Henry had been so much fun for her. He too, had been looking forward to the time when they would start their family. He had been raised in a large family. The oldest always had so much responsibility and he was always ready.

The weeks went by quickly planning for the baby. Henry made a crib and the rocking chair that Joseph's father had made was brought from the old cabin.

It was a time of joy as Rose's body grew larger. Blue Sky would check her frequently. Her size was becoming alarming to Blue Sky. She mentioned it to Rose but did not want to upset her.

The last month was especially hard for Rose. She complained how the baby was so active. She got no rest at all. Her nights were exactly like her days. The baby was moving and kicking, and she was not sleeping.

Blue Sky asked her to come into the hospital two weeks before the baby was due so Rose could get some rest, and Blue Sky could watch over her more closely.

Rose was at the hospital one week when her labor started. Blue Sky sent word to Henry he needed to come to the hospital as she thought the baby would be born that very night.

Everything went well even though it was a long night. A baby boy was born to Rose and Henry. Blue Sky cleaned the baby boy and laid him in Henry's arms. He held him safely and tenderly. His love for his wife and new son radiated from his face.

Rose suddenly began to moan and cried out in pain. Quickly Blue Sky checked Rose. It was then the unexpected happened, another baby.

Blue Sky found another baby was about to be born. Within minutes Rose gave birth to a baby girl. The baby girl's birth was fast and over in minutes. Blue Sky cleaned the tiny baby girl and wrapped her in a small warm soft cloth. Blue Sky could not hide the worried look on her face. This was a baby needing special care. Henry and Rose watched in silence as Blue Sky walked to the window and stood in a small amount of sunlight bringing the dawn of a new day.

Blue Sky lifted the tiny baby up over her head with her arms extended as high as she could and began to pray in a chant.

"Oh wonderful God of my people, send your living spirit, into the body of this girl. Let her live a long life with good health. Let her love and be loved. Let her live in harmony with all people." Then in a loud voice said, "Oh, living spirit, enter her body, now." The room was totally silent.

Blue Sky stood for a moment longer and the lamp behind her flickered and nearly went out before it grew bright again. She laid the baby in Henry's hand. She was the size of his hand. Henry looked down at his precious daughter and he swore to himself he would take care of his new special responsibility with all the love and strength he had. He laid the baby girl on Rose's chest. The warmth of Rose's skin would keep the baby warm.

Rose lay holding a big baby boy and his twin baby sister that was less than half his size. Tears willed up in Rose's eyes as she looked into the eyes of her beautiful daughter, with all of the love and compassion her heart could render.

Henry and Rose were completely overwhelmed. No one knew or had even suspected. One name had been talked about but now the decision of picking another name was needed. Paul was chosen for the baby boy, and Margaret was the name of the tiny girl.

⌒ Chapter 13 ⌒

Henry worked until he finished another crib exactly like the first one. The small pieces of wood from the new crib, was made into a box to put on top of the straw mattress. Henry padded the inside of the box. This was Margaret's new bed. No one was allowed to go into her room or pick her up except Rose or Henry. The busy days came and went in a hurry as the babies were always hungry. The clothes line was full all of the time.

The happiness Rose felt made all of the extra care with two babies much easier. Both babies were content and cried only when they were extremely hungry. Rose discovered the babies would sleep better if they were together in the same crib for their afternoon nap.

The feeding of Margaret was every two hours around the clock. Rose held her gently to her chest. Rose would open Margaret's little mouth with her finger and then feed her. It took over two weeks of the routine and then early one morning Rose awoke feeling uneasy. She listened needing to hear the sound again. She realized the sound was Margaret crying. Rose had not heard her cry this way. She hurried to the box and for the first time Rose understood the cry was Margaret indicating she was hungry. It took Margaret nine more months to catch up in weight to Paul's birth weight.

Maude was always willing to help whenever she was need-ed. She would ride her horse and just show up nearly every afternoon.

Maude was an older woman whose past had kept her in a state of depression and she carried a huge amount of guilt. Rose met Maude under desperate conditions, in both of their lives. Rose was being stocked by a dark-skinned man. Maude's life had been impaired by a terrible accident. The night Maude

---

shot her loving young husband brought on her own severe punishment of herself. It had been a terrible accident. Toby had brought the two women together in a time they unknowingly needed each other.

↷ Chapter 14 ↶

The twins were growing and were very lively. Maude loved to make cookies for them. She also loved to rock them. She held each one on her lap in the big rocking chair and would read to them. Each day passed fast with love and happiness in the cabin.

Rose had never been so happy and relaxed. She began to feel her body was changing again. Blue Sky confirmed Rose was again going to have a baby. Henry was elated with the new baby coming and told Rose, "I have a name for a baby girl. We'll wait and I'll tell you what it is when the baby is born. And, if it is a girl.

↷ Chapter 15 ↶

Henry had discussed a cattle herd for the pasture with Rose many times. Rose wanted one too. Her only concern was how he would drive a herd up from Texas alone. Henry explained he would send for all of his brothers or all of the brothers his father could spare at this time of the year. The brothers arrived as soon as the work was done at their home. They all came.

All of Henry's brothers sat on the top wooden board of the fence looking out over the pasture. They all wore faded jeans and worn out cowboy boots. They wore western hats with stains around the band. If you viewed them from the back you could not tell one brother from the other, except when you got to the brother sitting on the end holding onto the fence post. His clothes were the same as the brothers he loved. But his size was very noticeable. He sat straight as he could to look as tall as he could.

Thomas was determined not to be left behind.

Henry had told his brothers about his plan to go to Texas and bring home five hundred head of breeding cattle. They were all excited just talking about this large undertaking.

The brothers all told Henry, "We're all here, and we all want to go to help you bring your herd home."

Henry was sure his mother would not let Thomas go. He was the baby of her big family, and she could not stand to have something bad happen to him. Also the feeling she had, she explained several times. "When he grows up," which she knew he would, "I'll lose the feeling of being needed." Her sister had left him to love and raise, as if he were her own. He was only a baby when Thomas came into her family.

Thomas begged and pleaded. He did not want or would not be left at home, "with girls" as he put it.

The only way Henry's mother would even talk about Thomas going on the cattle drive was if Henry, along with each of the brothers promised to watch over him.

Thomas had been born premature because of an illness his mother developed. She lived long enough to give birth to him. His real mother was Henry's aunt. Three other small children along with Thomas came to live in the already full Helgen's home and Thomas with his three sisters became part of the family.

It took a lot of discussion before an agreement was made. Then after the agreement was made, each brother had to send a telegram to their mother and promise to watch over Thomas.

It was then and only then did Thomas's mother agree to let him go.

❧ Chapter 16 ☙

The next few days were spent preparing for the long trip. Each man had to have two rolled up blankets, one to lie on and one to cover up with. They each had to carry a poncho in case of rain, and one change of clothes. That was enough for the horse to carry.

Henry had given each one instructions he wanted carried out. "To get as many head safely home." He had said firmly.

Each cowhand had shaken Henry's hand telling him without saying a word they would do their very best to get the five hundred head of cows to Rose's pasture in Oklahoma.

Henry gave each of his nine brothers an extra squeeze as he shook their hand. The youngest of the brothers, eight-year-old Thomas would ride beside Henry. Henry would protect him at any cost.

⁓ Chapter 17 ⁓

They had spend many days rounding the cattle up and then the cows all had to counted. The cattle drive was about to start. Now it was time. Henry watched as the cattle started to move. The cowhands were all in place. Some hands stayed at the rear to make sure every cow was on the trail to Rose's land.

Henry had been watching the angry clouds building up over their heads but waiting would have meant losing another day, and his concern was only to get the cattle home to Oklahoma. The dust was thick at this time.

Henry looked up at the sky one more time as the cattle started to move. The breeze was pushing the dust up into the air almost making it impossible to see the sky. The cowhands watched as Henry's arm waved in the air. He was sending a message to start the cattle moving. The cattle moved out slowly.

Henry continued to turn completely around in his saddle and check on Thomas. When Thomas saw him looking toward him he would wave. Thomas was Henry's responsibility and he would go to any end to keep him safe.

The cowhands knew they would spend the entire day in the saddle. The cook had provided food for each man to carry in his saddlebag along with a canteen full of water.

Each man rode in their place surrounding the herd. Henry had planned the trip very carefully. Placing each cowhand so each one could just see the other off in the distance.

The cattle traveled many miles the first day. Late in the afternoon each man sent a signal to the closest man to slow the cattle down. Four men rode out in front of the fast moving cattle and slowed them down to a very slow pace. The cattle were extremely tired and eager to stop for the night.

The cook pulled his cook wagon half way on the outside of the herd. The men knew it would take the cook time to start a campfire and prepare their coffee. It gave the cattle time to stop, and some would lie down for the night. The cattle that lay down seemed to stop the nearest cows from moving on.

The cowhands took turns riding up to the cook wagon. Henry gave them only time to eat, drink coffee and visit about the day. Every other man would have night watch the first night and another man would stay awake the next night to protect the cattle from rustlers or wild animals.

When the night came, no stars could be seen. The clouds covered the heaven. The riders had to depend on their horse to see the way to the next rider.

The following morning breakfast was ready and each man ate until they were full even though Henry was trying to hurry everyone.

When Henry thought all of the cowhands were in place he raised his arm and the next man did the same. The herd had rested well in spite of the coyotes crying off in the distance. They headed the thirsty cattle toward a creek. Henry had planned they could get to it by noon. The closer they got to the water, the faster they traveled. Men rode on each side in several places. Henry and Thomas rode out in front to get the cows to follow.

The cattle all drank until they were full.

The dust could be seen for miles. It entered the air and raised high into the clouds.

The second night they traveled until almost dawn. Henry called out to the nearest man to slow down. Each man rode more to the front to slow the herd to a stop for rest. Henry guessed they had traveled about ten miles. The evening air felt cool. Each man slowly crawled down from their horses after riding for nearly twelve hours.

Each man was allowed two hours of sleep while Henry and Toby rode in each direction around the herd.

☞ Chapter 18 ☜

The men were all back on their horses the minute they woke to the sound of thunder and saw the lightening off in the distance. The cows began to move, showing signs of restlessness. The men knew just what to do in the morning. Half of the herd would start first. A few riders would ride between the cattle and start the other half to move.

The next creek was also welcome. The riders would move the first cows out and then the next half entered the creek. When all of the cattle had drank they herded the last ones together with the first half of the herd.

The days slipped by and each cowhand was thankful when the night hours came. If they were not on night watch, they lay on their bed roll and usually did not hear the cattle beller or any wild animal, sleeping soundly until morning.

The rain started slowly, and it looked as if the cattle were glad to stop breathing in the dust they all kicked up. The rain was gentle most of the morning and then it began to pour. Each man reached back of their saddle and slipped their ponchos on.

Henry sent word from one man back to the other they needed to keep going. If they stopped he thought the lightening and the thunder would spook the herd and start a stampede. During a lightening strike Henry looked back and could see Thomas hunched over riding just where he was supposed to be.

The men were all tired and hungry but they all knew Henry was right. Toby told the men exactly what Henry wanted them to do. The rain poured most of the night and the ground was soggy becoming hard for the herd and horses to walk on. Mud was sticking to their horse's hooves.

↷ *Chapter 19* ↶

It was just getting light out and they were approaching the last creek marking just another day's ride to Rose's land. It continued to rain and the temperature was dropping. The men were all cold and shivering from being wet.

Toby rode up beside Henry and yelled, "I can hear a horrible roaring noise Henry, we need to stop the cattle."

Henry yelled back above the roar of the bank full of rushing water, "We're too late to stop them now. Let them go and tell the men not to try and save any of them. We'll come back and round them up."

Rose's magnificent horse jumped into the rushing water and swam with the first group of cattle. Henry reached the bank and the horse leaped upon the ground. Some of the cattle had spread out afraid of jumping into the water.

What Henry saw next made him panic. He watched as Thomas went down into a deeper part of the creek to try and herd the cattle back up stream, forgetting what Henry and Toby had warned each man about the creek.

Thomas had only wanted to save the stray cattle. The creek dropped off fast. It was deeper than he had expected. The underlying current was very fast. And now with the rushing water on top, all of the water was a dangerous swirling pool. No one was safe in it.

Henry jerked his horse around and kicked him hard as they jumped into the water. Thomas' horse was fighting and kicking when Thomas fell from the saddle. Henry got Rose's horse as close as he could. The cattle Thomas tried to get across were all around them. Henry took a hold of his saddle horn and swung his leg over so he could slide down into the water to rescue Thomas. Henry had hold of Thomas' arm and struggled until he got Thomas' hand clamped around Rose's horse's stirrup and Thomas was dragged through the water onto the shore.

Henry was a very strong man but he was not a good swimmer. The cattle around him were kicking and suddenly he felt pain in his leg as he was kicked and he went under. The next kick caught him along his head. From then on he felt nothing.

He was under the water, but Thomas was safe.

∽ Chapter 20 ∾

What Henry did not know was he was being watched.

The water was churning in every direction. His body turned in a circling pool of water. In minutes he was released from the current and was pulled and pushed to the surface. His lungs were filling with water. Then his face emerged from the water and he gasped for air before going under again. Without any warning the currents horrific speed sent his body around a sharp bend. Henry was about to die.

Toby watched in stricken terror. Henry disappeared under the water. He screamed for every man to get out of the water. He was sure no man could survive in the flooded creek. He yelled, "No one else will die here today." All of the cowhands gathered together when the last of the herd crossed the deadly creek. Each man was suffering in their own way. They stood first looking at each other not believing, then as reality set in, no one spoke.

Toby knew he was in charge now. He spoke first, loud enough for every cowboy to hear, "I want you all to know no one is to blame. It was an accident. And I never want to hear anything different. We are taking the herd home as planned."

Thomas shifted his weight from one foot to the other and then nervously opened his mouth and said. "Toby, we can't go home without him." Then, wept unashamed as if his heart had broken. All of the cowhands encircled him and hugged him. Every man put their head down and cried.

Toby reached in his back pocket, took out a handkerchief, and wiped his face, then said, "When the water goes down, we'll all come back and find him."

⌒ Chapter 21 ⌒

The old man stepped out into the water. He knew exactly where he could stand. He also knew he had one chance and one chance only to grab the man that was being tossed and turned torturously and coming at him as fast as the current. He knew he had to grab a hold of whatever he could on the man's body, because if he missed, the man would die if he wasn't gone already.

On the bank an old woman with her arms extending out over the water was waiting. No one witnessed the rescue.

The old man spread his legs and feet apart and stood with the rushing water pushing with great force against his body. Then the body came at the old man nearly knocking him down. He tried to grab but the body slipped by him. His last grab was unbelievable. The old man had a hold of a pant cuff. He held on and took one small step at a time to the shore where the old woman was waiting. She reached out and took hold of the other leg and pulled with all of her strength to get both men out of the water.

The lifeless body lay between them. They both looked at a very young man. The old man turned the body on its side and pounded hard on his back. Then quickly turned him on his back and pushed on his chest. Then, turned him again on his side, and with an open hand slapped on his back. The water came gushing out of Henry's mouth and nose with spasms of coughing and choking.

The old woman muttered, "He's alive."

Henry was alive. He was unconscious, but Henry was alive.

Chapter 22

When water stopped coming from Henry's mouth and he stopped coughing, the old man and woman hooked their arms under each of Henry's arms and started dragging him away from the creek. His chin lay on his chest as they pulled him along. They would stop every so often and rest.

It was nearly dark before they reached the settlement.

The big white square house was on the edge of a small town. They entered from the back. They took one step at a time pulling Henry into a back porch and then into an unused bedroom located in the extreme corner of the house. They lifted his unconscious body up on top of a bed.

The old woman hurried to light a lamp. She lay out a flannel nightgown and left closing the door.

The room had a bed, dresser and an old trunk. The dresser had a wash basin and a bar of lye soap setting on it. The walls had pictures of Wilber and Dora's parents. They were the founders of this old settlement and were well known. They owned the general store, feed store, harness shop and the bank.

Now Wilber and Dora Kolveck owned the entire town.

They never had to work because their parent's money took care of them. The town people called them spinsters. They were always alone. No one came to see them. People were always envious.

This was just what they needed. Henry came into their lives just at the right time.

In the kitchen Dora skimmed off the broth from the soup she had already prepared for their supper.

Wilber removed all of Henry's cold wet clothes and dressed him in his night gown. He lay Henry between the sheet blankets and covered him with several home made quilts to warm him.

Dora put the broth in a cup. Wilber raised Henry's head so he could drink the hot broth without choking.

The lamp was blown out and they went to their own rooms. The day had been hard work for the two of them. Now, they would divide up the work. The old man would take care of Henry's personal needs, and the old woman would take care of the food.

Wilber and Dora Kolveck would have something to do. It would be their very own SECRET.

The big white house was built many years ago by their parents. The years had slipped away and they remained living in the house after their parents had passed away. Wilber and Dora had grown old without marrying. Dora was ten years older and had always made most of the decisions. But this decision, Wilber had made.

Wilber was up at the break of dawn and went directly to check on his new friend. He had finally found someone of his own.

He took good care of Henry and Dora fed him. Wilber talked to Henry as if he were awake and would answer. The only thing he did not do, was, cut Henry's hair nor did he shave him.

∝ Chapter 23 ∾

The two little children were clapping, jumping and running to the windows as the first of the cattle herd came on to Henry and Rose Donlin Helgens' land. The gates were all open and the first man on horseback led them into the green lush pasture.

Rose was as elated as her little children. Henry was home and the baby she was carrying was coming soon.

Rose could see the first horse leading the cattle was her beautiful giant horse. Then she could see Thomas riding her horse, not Henry, who she had expected. She stood with her eyes fixed on her horse.

Rose watched as Thomas led the first of the cattle into the south pasture and then she watched him ride toward the bunkhouse. She wondered why he had not ridden back to help his brothers and the rest of the cowhands bring the remaining herd.

After Rose put the children down for their nap, she hugged her babies tenderly and kissed them over and over. The feeling of fear was making her heart beat faster. It wasn't like Henry not to come into the cabin as soon as he arrived home. She had seen the cowhands gather at the gate, but none came into the cabin. Not even Toby. They stood talking with their heads down.

She slipped out of the cabin and headed straight to the bunkhouse as fast as her burdensome uncomfortable body could walk.

Opening the door as quietly as she could, she stepped in and closed the door behind her.

Rose walked in a few feet and stopped as she heard a muffled sound. She took a couple more steps and she could see Thomas' bunk bed. He had insisted he get to sleep where his brothers did.

At the foot of Thomas' bed burrowed under all of his blankets. Rose could hear sobs, sniffling and gasping for air. It was as if all of the worst nightmares she had in her young life were now coming true.

She gently pulled the covers back and sat on the bed. Rose reached over and pulled Thomas up over her swollen body. He clung to her forgetting about her body and the baby coming.

While hugging him, she remembered the little boy who had sat next to her pillow and leaning over had kissed her when she was recovering in Henry's home.

With a voice almost inaudible, Thomas whispered, "I'm so sorry Rose I just tried to save the strays."

Rose said, "Thomas, I would like you to come to the cabin and stay with me and the children."

"Thomas, please don't tell me anything. Henry is alive."

"No, Rose," Thomas wanted to tell her.

Interrupting him, Rose said, "Thomas, you and I are gong to find him. Henry's baby is coming soon. When I am ready, we will find him. He's alive. He's waiting to be found."

∽ Chapter 24 ∾

The day dragged by as the yelling from the cowhands continued until the last of the herd went through the gate and into the pasture. Margaret and Paul waited for their father to come into the cabin and eat supper with them. Finally, Rose fed the twins and put them into their bed. Their father didn't come, and they were sound asleep in a short time.

She stood in front of the window in the kitchen washing the dishes the twins used, while thinking she needed to send for Blue Sky soon. Blue Sky and Rose were more than good friends. They had something between them. It was a bond. They concealed a hidden secret that each one knew the other would never reveal. Rose respected and trusted Blue Sky. She had seen her deliver many difficult births. The secret came to Rose when thinking of her own baby's birth coming soon.

It was a year ago in the Higgins' Hospital during a terrible rain storm, two baby boys were born. A baby boy born to a very young, unknown girl. The baby was strong and healthy. At the same time, Rose friend, Mary Rocker gave birth to a still born baby boy.

The young girl did not survive. She died that night giving birth.

Rose Donlin made the decision to switch the babies with only one other person knowing, Blue Sky. Rose knew Blue Sky would never betray her.

Mary did not know. She named her new baby boy, Hank, in honor of Henry.

⌒ *Chapter 25* ⌒

The loud knock on the door interrupted her thoughts. It was like someone was pounding on the door. Rose took a step toward the door and then her chest tightened up. Severe pain ripped through her body making her bend over to catch her breath . Her body was preparing for the birth of her baby.

The door opened and standing on her front porch was Toby, Rufus George and Sheriff Les. Before anyone said a word, Rose could see the sad look each man had on his face.

Rose spoke first saying, "Toby, please go get Blue Sky."

Then she said to Rufus George, "Take the twins and Thomas to Maude, she knows they are coming to stay for a few days. Also take the cardboard box with their clothes in it."

She looked at Sheriff Les and said, "Whatever you came to tell me it will have to wait as Henry's baby is coming. Please come into the kitchen and have a cup of coffee."

Rose turned and walked to her bedroom. She slipped into her nightgown. Prepared the bed and laid on Henry's side of their bed holding his pillow tight to her chest. The smell of Henry was on it.

Toby's horse galloped all of the way to Blue Sky's home. He jumped from his horse and ran into her cabin forgetting to knock. He grabbed Blue Sky by the arm and said in a loud, unlike his own voice, "Rose is having her baby." Blue Sky always had her bag packed ahead when she was to deliver a baby.

In Blue Sky's bag was a special tea from a root she grew in her backyard. It would be given to Rose to drink just before the baby was born. It had a numbing effect from the waist down.

Mary reached Rose's cabin minutes before Blue Sky. Elizabeth, Sarah and Hank were left for the hospital cook to watch until Rose's baby was born. Mary always had women at the hospital to watch her children, especially Hank. The baby boy was born on a very stormy night a little over a year ago.

Rose had placed a baby boy in Mary's arms and told her, "You have a healthy boy."

Mary did not know the whole truth. She loved the boy she thought she had given birth. Elizabeth and Sarah thought Hank belonged to them. They loved him dearly.

Rose looked up and said, "Something awful has happened to Henry. But no one must tell me until this baby is born."

Mary nodded and wet a cloth in cold water and wiped Rose's face. She wanted to care for Rose like Rose had cared for her when her son Hank had been born.

Everyone knew about Henry but no one would tell Rose until after the baby was born.

Blue Sky was nearly out of breath when she got to Rose's bed. A brief examination showed Blue Sky she needed to give Rose the tea. Blue Sky mixed the special tea and Rose was eager to drink it all. The room was very quiet. Blue Sky gave Rose her instructions, and only minutes went by before the baby girl's first cry.

Mary wrapped the baby in a blanket and walked to the kitchen for Sheriff Les to see. The first question he asked was, "What did Rose name her?"

Her answer was, "Baby Girl." Henry had a name but told Rose, "It will be a surprise until we know it's a girl."

Mary asked Sheriff Les to please come back in the morning to tell Rose about Henry. Blue Sky had given Rose one more cup of tea and Rose was asleep.

Sheriff Les stood up and said, "Tell Rose I'll be here early in the morning."

❧ Chapter 26 ❧

The morning came too soon but he knew what he had to do. Sheriff Les arrived at Rose's cabin as the sun started to rise.

Rose had just fed her new baby girl. Blue Sky answered the door and asked Sheriff Les to come in. She gave him a hot cup of coffee and went to tell Rose he was here.

Rose sat down across from Sheriff Les and looked at him as if she were not even seeing him.

"Rose," the Sheriff said. "There has been a terrible accident." He stopped to draw in a deep breath and then said, "Its

Henry, Rose. Henry drowned in the awful torrential flood we had."

Rose never cried. She looked directly at Sheriff Les and said, "He could have survived, maybe he's lying along the bank, hurt. Why aren't you out looking for him? He's alive, Sheriff Les, find him."

"No, Rose. No one could have survived what he went through. Toby, along with all of Henry's brothers, said he could never have survived. They saw him go under."

"You must not tell me how it happened, not yet. But, Sheriff Les, he's alive. I can feel him. Please find him." She stood up and walked to her bedroom saying, "He's alive."

Blue Sky stayed with Rose at night. In the morning nothing had changed. Rose did not cry, nor could she cry.

The men stayed away from the cabin. The usual laughing and talking from the bunkhouse was silent now.

Several of Henry's brothers rode by the cabin, and Rose knew they were going out to search for Henry. No one looked toward the cabin.

The baby girl was welcomed by all of the friends Henry and Rose had. But they found it was hard to be overjoyed with a dark cloud hanging over the community's head. They left the cabin in silence

⁂ Chapter 27 ⁂

In the week that followed, Rose sent word she would like her horse hitched up to the buggy. Every cowhand wanted to do all they could for her. She also asked a different one of Henry's brothers to come into the cabin and watch the children. Rose would feed the twins and lay them down for a nap. Baby girl would be fed and when she was asleep, Rose and Thomas would slip out of the cabin and ride toward the creek. They rode along it and then would stop the buggy, then walk, searching for her beloved.

Each day a different brother came in and each day, she and Thomas searched going further.

Everyone knew she would have to give up when the snow started to fall. No one wanted to tell her.

When Rose was well enough to ride her magnificent horse, she and Thomas would ride out and walk the bank of the creek. Some times she would go down into the creek and look very carefully. She was so afraid she would miss footsteps or perhaps a piece of torn clothing. She would lift up and look under the long grass leaning over the bank. She thought he could have gotten hurt and was lodged in a small spot in the debris.

The days were long and tiresome, and she knew time was running out for her to find her Henry. Also, her son and two daughters needed her.

The next afternoon Rose had taken care of the children and laid them down for their nap. Thomas was out in the yard behind the cabin playing with Pal.

John Fitzpatrick knocked on her cabin door. She let him in and poured coffee and he sat across from her and never took his eyes off of her. She mentioned she would prefer not to talk about Henry, and he politely obeyed her request.

First, she did not want John to even talk about her Henry.

He appeared more interested in talking about her. He asked what she was going to do now if she needed help to run the cattle ranch.

Rose's reply was, "I have all of Henry's brothers working here."

That was when she made the decision to hire a full time housekeeper, so at no time would she be alone with any man, especially John Fitzpatrick.

◌ Chapter 28 ◌

Rose wrote an ad and delivered it to the Oklahoma City newspaper. Stating she would like an older woman to live in and help with her children.

A lady showed up at the cabin a few days later. Rose opened the door and a tall, stout, full figured woman that a baby would love to lay against was standing in the doorway. Rose opened her mouth to speak and before she could, the woman said, with an accent, "I've come to take care of your young babies. I can cook, clean and sew, and I can ride a horse. Her hands were large indicating to Rose she could do all of the things she said she could do. Her speech was with a German accent. Her light brown hair was pulled back into a large knot. It had a small amount of grey on the area near her ears.

Her dress was starched and clean. It was flowered print with an apron over it, hanging to her ankles.

Rose took a deep breath and said, "Come in, please, and tell me your name."

"My name is Inga Schmit. I have no family here, my parents sent me from Germany to make money to send to them." Without stopping she said, "My dear young woman, you look peeked. Let me work and help you."

↶ Chapter 29 ↷

Six long months had passed, and Rose continued to search. Each afternoon she and Thomas left to search the creek. They had traveled up to the sharp bend that took the creek around and away from the settlement. She mentioned to Thomas they would travel into town the next day.

The following day she and Thomas rode into Main Street and stopped in front of the stable. Rose's attention was drawn to a sign at the opening of Main Street.

It read KOLVECK SETTLEMENT. YOU WILL BE FIRMLY PROSECUTED IF YOU CAUSE ANY TROUBLE.

Rose asked if the stable hand would feed and water her giant horse. The stable man stood admiring Rose's horse when she asked if he had seen a stranger in his town. He answered quickly, "Can't say I have ma'am but you can ask at the boarding house or the eating place across the street. The general store is another place you could ask although we don't get too many new people in this town. Our town is owned by one family. They live in the big white house on the edge of town."

Rose thanked him and paid for the care he had given her horse.

She and Thomas walked into the boarding house. The man behind the desk was leaning back in his chair asleep. He woke with a surprised look on his face.

"I'm looking for a young man. He could have come into your town and he could have been injured." Rose said with firmness in her voice.

The man answered saying, "Ma'am you need to see the Doc. He could have treated him. His office is upstairs over the general store. He is always there.

Rose's Unexpected Tragedy

Rose touched Thomas' shoulder so he would follow her to the door. The stairs leading to the Doc's office were on the outside of the building. The sign over his office door read Dr's Office---Dr. Albert.

Rose knocked lightly. No one answered, Thomas knocked loudly. A male voice answered sounding agitated. "Come in, and don't break my door down." Thomas opened the door and stepped in front of Rose who was now a step behind. The elderly man sat at his desk. Rose noticed a small flask standing in the corner of his desk.

His first words sounded a little slurred, "What can I do for you young man?"

"No, no, not me, my brother is missing and he could have been hurt. Maybe you saw him." Thomas said. Rose didn't think she would ever hear Thomas say there was a chance Henry was still alive. And she thought he sounded angry.

"No," the doctor answered slowly after he swallowed hard. "I have not seen any stranger. How was your brother hurt?"

"When the creek," Thomas began, "outside of this town was full after the rain, my brother fell into the water. He could have been hurt, maybe scratched up by the limbs and logs washed in from shore."

Dr. Albert said, "The only person I have treated recently that was hurt from skin scratches was Wilber Kolveck. He came in and asked for some medicine for tears on his arms and legs. I put salve on his open areas which I didn't think he needed all of the bottles of salve he asked to take home with him. He and his sister own the town, so naturally I sent the number of bottles with him that he asked for. I haven't seen him since." He paused as if thinking out loud. Then he said, "Maybe, I should go out and check on him."

~ Chapter 30 ~

After Wilber began talking to Henry about his lonely life, Henry continued listening with his eyes closed. When Wilber turned to close the door, Henry opened his eyes and looked around the room. He closed his eyes again and did not open them again until Wilber left the room.

Wilber helped him up on the commode next to the bed. Then gave Henry his bath and later laid him safely back into his bed. Wilber talked the entire time. Mostly about how no one liked him when he grew up. How the kids picked on him. How Dora would beat them up to protect him.

The light knock on the door meant Dora was bringing Henry's breakfast. Dora proceeded to feed Henry and was kind and gentle and also quiet because Wilber told her not to talk to his new companion. Henry was his friend, and no one would ever take him away from him. Dora would never cross Wilber. She knew how vicious he could get if he became angry. Wilber was short and overweight, and Dora was tall and thin. It had always been a problem between them. Dora was ten years old when Wilber was born. She doted on him as did their parents. It didn't take him but a few years to realize he could do whatever he wanted to at home. When they went to school or into town, he expected Dora to watch over and protect him. Dora's life became a living hell.

Since Henry had been in their home, Wilber had been happier than Dora had ever seen him. She would not do anything to change this.

⚘ Chapter 31 ⚘

Wilber became a little agitated if he saw Henry respond in anyway. He wanted complete control. One morning Henry moved and Wilber yelled, "You lay still."

It was nearly six months and Henry was waking up each morning now in a tormented state. He had no idea where he was. He tried to understand what Wilber was saying. He could not remember who he was. He wanted to say his name but nothing came into his mind. For the first time since he opened his eyes, he knew something was very wrong.

Henry was having feelings. He felt something strange was going on. He had never been in a prison but he was feeling as if he were a prisoner. He knew he had to lie very still when Wilber was in the room and also keep his eyes closed.

Wilber and Dora had gone to their room. With only a small amount of light in his room, Henry raised his head and looked around. He did not recognize anything in the room, then he noticed directly across from his bed a small amount of light coming from a small round coin sized hole in the wall.

The house was old and the floors were made with wide wooden boards. They were old now and dry. He could hear the floor squeak outside of his room. He quickly laid his head down on his feather pillow. Henry raised his head a few minuets later only about an inch off of his pillow. The light was gone from the small opening. He was sure something moved outside the hole. He could not understand anything that was happening here.

⌒ Chapter 32 ⌒

Rose thanked the doctor and then stopped and said, "If you go out to the big white house, please ask if they have seen anyone new in their area. If they have I would like to know. Thomas and I will come back in a few days. Also tell them we'll stop and see them soon."

The doctor knew Wilber and Dora would never let anyone into their home, even just to visit. No one ever went there unless they had a special reason. He would have to go and see the Kolveck's before Rose and Thomas arrived at their door.

It was late in the day as Rose and Thomas left the doctor's office and headed home.

After Rose and Thomas left the office, the doctor took several drinks. He thought about a rumor he had heard once about a man drifting through town and the man had stopped at the big white house and no one had ever seen him again.

⌒ Chapter 33 ⌒

Rose, with Thomas, sitting behind her on her horse, rode directly up to the cabin. Inga opened the cabin door. She had a big smile on her face and was so excited to tell Rose, Baby Girl was able to crawl. Henry's daughter slowly crawled along the floor. She was as strong and determined as her father had always been.

Margaret and Paul had encouraged Baby Girl to crawl and now, Inga told Rose the twins would stand her up to a chair and tell her to "hang on."

Rose wanted Henry here more than ever. He was missing out on so much in their life now.

⫷ Chapter 34 ⫸

Henry woke in a sweat. It was still dark out. He had one bad dream after another, waking after each one. He tried to remember wanting to know what they meant.

He turned onto his side for the first time then remembered he was being watched and turned back so no one in the house would see he could do this. Even in his confusion, he was beginning to feel fear.

Henry heard the boards squeak. His day was about to start all over again. He closed his eyes tight and waited fearing one of Wilber's outbursts.

Wilber was very strong. He could lift Henry up out of bed, stand him on his feet. He would turn him to set on a commode.

Dora brought a pan of warm water in for Wilber to bathe Henry. Dora left without speaking to get Henry's breakfast as usual. The breakfast was the same every morning and the small amount was the same. Dora always cooked the oatmeal until it was hard and dry. She carried the oatmeal into the back of the big white house to the unused bedroom, until now.

Wilber was talking as usual. Henry acted the same as he did the first day. He listened intently wanting to figure out who he was and why he was here.

Henry's dreams were different each night and yet they were the same. They were different because he would see more people each night. He did not know why a cabin with two little children sitting on the roof came twisting and turning floating down a river. Each night as the cabin came rushing by him, there were more people looking out of each window.

In one window was a young man. In the next window was a very large colored man. Then he would wake up in a state of panic with his head hurting.

His night shirt was wet from sweat. He couldn't move.

Morning came and the day was agonizing for Henry not knowing or understanding what was happening to him.

Wilber opened Henry's door and pushed a large old rocking chair in the room. Henry tried not to open his eyes. He did not want Wilber to become irritated at him. Wilber lost his temper over very small things. He would yell at Henry and blame him if something went wrong for him.

Dora was so thankful they had found Henry. She would not have to take the wrath of Wilber's temper. She could go to her room and forget about him for awhile.

Wilber prepared Henry for his day. He told Henry, "I'll let you sit up in the rocking chair if you do not try to stand up." Henry made no indication that he even heard. But he heard every word.

The rocking chair was placed by a window. At first, while Wilber was in the room Henry held his eyes closed and his head remained down. Wilber moved Henry to the rocking chair. He felt Wilber's hand around his waist. Wilber was tying him in the rocking chair. But why?

The sun looked so bright outside and shined in on him. It was so good to feel the warm sun rays on his body. He had lain in the bed for what seemed forever. He would move around in his bed when the hole in the wall was dark.

⌒ Chapter 35 ⌒

With his back to the hole in the wall, Henry felt safe in opening his eyes and it was so wonderful for him to be able to look outside. For the first time in a very long time he looked at green grass and beautiful trees. He could see hills. His mind was trying to sort this all out. Then for the first time in many months he saw a bird. He watched it soar in the air and he realized the bird was free. While he was watching the bird something else came into view.

He could see a young woman on a beautiful dark horse. She had long blond colored hair. Behind her sitting on the back of her horse was a young dark haired boy. The horse was coming toward him.

Just then he heard the floor boards squeak behind him in the hall. He knew someone was coming in a hurry. Wilber opened the door, and in seconds he was standing next to Henry. Henry closed his eyes. Wilber reached around Henry's waist and quickly untied the rope. Wilber pulled Henry roughly up out of the rocking chair and almost carried him to the bed. Once he had Henry in bed he covered him clear up to his eyes with a quilt.

Wilber was mad and mumbling very nasty words. He left the room, slamming the door behind him. Henry heard the door lock. Henry did not get supper that night. Something had happened in the house but he did not know what

ᴄ◦ *Chapter 36* ◦ᴐ

Rose tied her horse up to the hitching post outside of the big white house. The knock on the front door brought Dora hurrying before Wilber got to the door first.

Dora opened the door only enough to see a young woman standing there. Rose could see only half of Dora's face. Her face looked pale and showed wrinkles from age. Rose thought she looked sad especially when she whispered.

Rose thought this was all very strange.

Rose asked if Dora had seen a stranger pass by a few months ago.

"No, no, I did not," Dora answered. "What is he to you?" Her voice was getting softer.

Rose said slowly, "He is my husband."

"Do you have children?" Dora whispered so Wilber could not hear. "What is his name?"

"Yes, yes, we have three." Rose said then added quickly, "His name is Henry Helgens."

Dora heard Wilber move his feet behind her. She instantly said loudly, "No, no, we have not seen anyone." She started to close the door.

Rose said, as she grabbed to stop Dora from shutting the door. "You said, we, who else lives in the house with you?" Of course, Rose had heard from all the towns store owners a brother and sister lived in the big white house.

"Are you living here alone?" Rose wanted to get an answer.

"Yes," then quickly added. "No, no, I live here with my brother."

Rose tried to keep Dora talking. "What is your brother's name?"

Although Rose couldn't see, from the back of the door, a hand pushed and slammed the door shut making a loud bang.

Rose turned and walked to her horse. Her mind was going over the conversation. Over the strange way Dora looked and why she would not let Rose in. Why did she abruptly slam the door?

The ride home for Rose was lonely and depressing. She felt sick to her stomach. She had been hopeful. She wanted so badly to hear good news.

◌ Chapter 37 ◌

Wilber was furious at Dora. He began yelling at her, "You told that woman too much. You should not have opened the door." His voice sounded mean and gravelly. And then he continued with a frown and a look of disapproval on his face.

"Do not open the door if she comes back. Do you hear me?" He said scornfully.

"Yes, Wilber, I hear you." Dora said as she left him standing there with a red face from having a temper tantrum and went into her room closing her bedroom door.

Wilber did not go into Henry's room that night and Henry was relieved.

The hole in the hall looked dark all night. Henry felt safe moving around in his bed. He fell asleep feeling helpless. His sleep was fitful. For a few hours he slept quietly.

Then the nightmares began.

The cabin bobbed up and down in the fast moving raging water. The same faces looked at him out of the windows.

Suddenly the nightmare changed and he was dreaming that the young woman he had seen outside his window was standing at the foot of his bed. She was smiling at him. She was dressed in a white dress. She had a pink silk ribbon in her hair.

He woke pushing his covers off and started to get up but she had vanished. Henry realized it was a dream. He was alone. No one was in his room.

For the first time, he felt sadness and he did not know why. He began to cry while pulling the covers up and over his head.

☙ Chapter 38 ❧

Rose lay in bed that night and her mind would not rest. She couldn't stop felling she needed to go back to the big white house.

What was going? Why did Dora whisper? Why did she act frightening? Rose was wondering why that house was drawing her to it.

It was nearly morning when she finally fell into a deep sleep.

⌒ Chapter 39 ⌒

Wilber got to the door before Henry heard the floor squeak. He threw open the door making Henry jerk. Wilber walked toward the bed while talking to himself but this time he was whispering so Henry could not hear what he was saying. He pulled Henry out of bed, sat him on the commode.

A light tap on the door and Dora came in with a pan of warm water.

"Get his breakfast now." Wilber screamed at her. Then added, "Get ready, we're leaving for the hunting lodge now. Don't light any lamps."

"No, no. Wilber, no" Dora begged.

The icy stare he gave her told her nothing was going to stop him.

Henry was fed his breakfast faster than ever before. Then Wilber slipped him into a warm buffalo coat. The big fur hat was placed on his head which nearly covered his face.

Dora slipped out of the back of the house and headed for the barn to harness the horses. She hitched the team to a wagon and drove up to the back steps of the big white house. Wilber laid Henry on the floor of the wagon while Dora locked up the house. She packed as much food as fast as she could so Wilber would not leave without her.

Wilber started the horses to move making Dora run along the side until her hand grabbed the seat to pull herself up.

If anyone saw them all they could see was the two of them. The trip would take most of the day.

Wilber whipped the horses unmercifully. At times Dora shut her eyes while hanging on with all of her strength. Wilber wanted to get to the cabin in the woods before it got dark. Henry had never had a ride like the ride he had in the wagon.

His whole body felt bruised. He did not even know the direction he was being taken.

Henry could see they were traveling in a forested area. Looking up at the thick area of trees made him think he had been in areas before with many trees. He tried to remember the last time he had seen so many trees. He closed his eyes and he pictured lying on a blanket, but a girl was there. He tried hard to see her face. Her hair was light-colored. Then he thought about when he was looking out of the window. The girl on the horse, she also had light-colored hair.

Just then Henry felt the horses start to slow down. He could hear tree branches hitting the side of the wagon. The trail they were on now sounded as if they were driving on weeds, brush and rocks. The wagon ride was becoming more rough, more uncomfortable for Henry. He was being jostled around.

Wilber had been quiet most of the trip. Now he was shouting orders at Dora.

Henry listened to Wilber yell, "I'll take the man into the cabin. You get the horses and wagon into the shed."

"His name is Henry." Dora said quietly.

"Don't tell me what to call him. I'll call him what I want to," Wilber corrected her as usual.

⌁ Chapter 40 ⌁

Henry was able to walk into the cabin with Wilber holding on to him. Wilber left the buffalo coat and fur hat on Henry until the cabin was warm. The cabin was extremely small so it only took a short time, and it was warm.

Wilber ordered Dora to bring in more wood from the huge wood pile. Then he said, "When you have wood in, you can get us something to eat."

He laid Henry on a bed next to the fireplace. The bed had a straw mattress. Henry closed his eyes while Wilber was near. Wilber was talking to himself, saying, "No one will ever find you now. No one will be able to find you."

Henry opened his eyes slightly and looked around. It looked so familiar and the mattress felt like another mattress he had slept on before. This was like another cabin.

Dora had their meal ready. For the first time Henry wanted to pick up and hold his own spoon to eat. Before he could, Wilber had it in his hand and full of mush.

Henry woke the next morning hearing Dora whispering, "How long are we staying here?"

"Wilber, he's married with three small children." There was a long silence before Wilber answered, "We're not ever going back.

∝ Chapter 41 ∞

Thomas was up first, taking care of Pal, the family dog. Rose and Inga greeted each other warmly in the kitchen while preparing breakfast. Margaret and Paul were always so happy to see their mother. The hugs and kisses were plentiful. Baby Girl stretched and yawned as Rose picked her up from her crib.

Rose hugged Baby Girl and began to cry. It was almost seven months since Henry disappeared and for the first time she was feeling doubt about Henry being alive. He had vanished and left nothing indicating he could still be alive. She looked at her daughter and thought of finding a name for her.

But then thought maybe she would wait a little longer.

After the kitchen was cleaned up, Inga took the children into their bedroom to read to them. Rose wondered if Margaret, Paul and Baby Girl would grow up reading and talking with a German accent. Now it did not matter.

Rose slipped out the back door and walked toward the bunkhouse. Before entering she knocked loudly on the door.

She heard several loud shouts to "Come in."

All of Henry's brothers had stayed and worked with the oil wells and helped Toby with the cattle. Henry had planned ahead just when the baby calves would be born. The care of all the cowherd was Toby's now. He knew exactly what Henry's plans were, "To have baby calves when the weather turned warm."

As Rose opened the door she yelled out, "It's Rose."

She could hear, "Damn it, where's my pants?" Rose took two steps very slowly. The brothers were all surprised to see her. If she wanted them, she would always send word for each one to come to the cabin and have coffee with her.

This was different. This was urgent. She felt this was her very last real hope.

They all stood in an awkward silence, Rose, especially.

She was going to ask them to break the law by breaking into the big white house.

Her eyes looked at each brother and then said, "I have one hope left and I'm asking you when it's dark this evening to help me break into a house. Rose explained in detail how Dora had acted and everything she had wanted to know about Henry, How inquisitive she was and then how she had slammed the door.

No one hesitated. They all wanted to help. A plan was made. The equipment they needed would be loaded on a wagon and as soon as the sun went down, they would be ready.

Thomas and Rose rode ahead. The rest rode in twos a distance apart. The wagon would be last.

Rose walked up to the front of the house while the brothers rode around to the back of the house. She knocked several times. The house was completely dark. Suddenly the front door opened and one of Henry's brothers said, "Come in, Rose," as he reached out for her hand. He had a funny little smile on his face. Her heart began to pound hard in her chest. He led her through the well kept house to the very last room. All nine of Henry's brother's were in the room and Thomas stepped in behind Rose.

They all stood looking at her.

The brother in age next to Henry said, "Rose, he's been here. He was definitely here."

Rose's body was trembling and she looked terrified. She knew now they had left because she had stopped at the house.

They had been in a hurry to leave. They had left behind the one thing Henry carried with him in his pocket everywhere.

His father's pocket watch with the fob hooked to his overall. It had stopped running but it was his. Three bowls sat on the table in the kitchen.

Rose's legs gave out and she slipped to the floor. The brothers lifted her on to the bed. She buried her face in the pillow, and she could smell the scent of her Henry.

Every inch of the house and barn was searched. They found the hole in the wall where he had been watched.

Thomas tapped Rose's shoulder and she looked into a face with a smile on it with eyes open wide. He said, "I found a picture of a hunting lodge. On the front, it read Kolveck Hunting Lodge. The both knew it was the name of the settlement that Wilber and Dora owned. They owned every business in the settlement and they owned the big white house. They also owned a hunting lodge.

⌒ Chapter 42 ⌒

Toby wanted to be the one to ride into the settlement. No one there knew him or had ever seen him in town. It was agreed they would all go back to Rose's homestead and wait for Toby to come back.

The house was locked up, and everything placed back as they had found it. They all arrived home with a few hours to sleep before dawn.

Toby knocked lightly on Rose's door. He explained he could not sleep before leaving for the Kolveck settlement.

They sat quietly whispering while having a cup of coffee. Rose told him about talking with the man at the stable and the man in the boarding house. She also mentioned Dr. Albert and where he was located.

She added, "I think he knows all about the two Kolvecks." Toby stood up and walked to the door. Then turned and said, "Rose, I promise I'll find out where they have taken Henry."

"Oh, Toby, nothing would make me happier. If only they haven't hurt him." Rose said sadly.

"Rose, Toby paused and continued. "If they were going to hurt him, they would have done it already in the house. Why would they sneak him out during the night? No, I think they have him for another reason but I don't know what it is"

Rose wanted to cry as Toby closed the door behind him, but no tears came as she put her head down to pray.

∽ *Chapter* 43 ∾

Henry wanted to get up out of bed; he knew he could. Wilber was asleep a few feet away, and Henry also knew he would be viciously punished.

Henry's night had brought a clear picture to him. The cabin he had seen nightly being pushed down the rapid creek was now setting on a piece of land surrounded by many trees. The cabin had a wrap around porch. A large old rocking chair was setting in one room.

He woke feeling agitated, not knowing whose cabin it was.

Wilber was yelling at Dora as soon as he woke. "Get more wood in, start the fireplace and get breakfast ready."

Dora answered softly, "Yes, Wilber," She did not want him unhappy. Dora hurried to accomplish all of her chores.

The oatmeal tasted good to Henry because she didn't cook it a long time like she did at the house and she knew Wilber wanted it now.

After Henry's morning care, Wilber sat him on an old leather couch. Wilber sat down beside him and appeared to be relaxed and began to talk about how his life had changed. "I have you. You listen to me and you're not like Dora. She tells me what to do all of the time."

Wilber turned to look directly at him and said, in a low voice so Dora could not hear him. "Is your name Henry?"

Henry wanted to answer. First, he did not know his name. Second, if he said something, would Wilber lash out at him? Wilber explained, "We will call you Henry."

The long day was over, and Henry lay in his bed going over and over in his mind what he remembered. Wilber told him his name was Henry. The cabin with the wrap around porch had green grass and large trees around it. He remembered the people in the windows of the cabin, the two little children who looked exactly like each other, the beautiful young woman that stood at the foot of his bed.

Henry's mind was working so hard his body became exhausted and without realizing, he drifted willingly off to sleep. Within minutes he was inside of the cabin, it was his cabin. The two little children were sleeping in cribs. The young beautiful woman turned and looked at him. His body was sweating. He raised his head to see her more clearly.

She spoke his name, "Henry."

His mouth opened and in his dream he said, "Rose."

His head was reeling with questions. He woke immediately, and he couldn't remember her name. He again went over all of his dreams. He knew he was beginning to remember small parts of his life. He also knew he could not let Wilber find out.

∽ Chapter 44 ∾

Rose had insisted Pal, her dog, go with Toby. Pal could bark and warn Toby if danger was near. She also gave him her loaded revolver that she had taken from Joseph.

Toby rode especially slow. The sun was coming up but he did not want to ride into the Kolveck settlement before the stable was open.

On the ride, his mind went back to seeing Henry's body going under in the fast white rapid water. He wanted to think and believe Henry was alive. If he was alive he promised Rose and himself he would not return home unless he brought Henry home to Rose and their family.

Toby looked up as he rode under the sign Rose had told him about. He also noticed the sign over each store.

The stable hand looked up and watched Toby swing his leg slowly over his horse.

Toby had not shaved or combed his hair. He wore dirty jeans and his boots were old and scuffed.

He greeted the worker and asked, "Would you water and feed my horse? I wonder if I can have some water for my dog. Also I would like to buy a horse from you."

"What are you doing with your rifle? You can't have a gun in this town," the stable hand was talking loud as if he wanted anyone watching to know so he would not get into trouble talking to someone carrying a gun in town.

"I came here to find a hunting lodge my father used to talk about. I want to go hunting. He told me if I got here to this town, someone would direct me to the lodge. He said he and the owner of the lodge hunted together." Toby was doing and saying all he could to convince him.

"Well, I really don't know for sure, I've heard people talk about it. Old Dr. Albert could likely tell you."

"About that horse you want to buy. I do have one and I'll even throw in a saddle blanket. That'll be $300.00," the stable man said with a slight smile on his face.

Toby looked at the horse and knew it was only worth about $25.00. Rose had given him plenty of money and had said, "Toby, spend it all to get Henry back."

"Ok," Toby said. He gave him the money and asked where he could find Dr. Albert. Also, the general store to buy food for camping.

Pal stood up and stretched as Toby mounted his horse. He rode leading the other horse. He stopped first to purchase food and another bedroll for the extra horse.

Toby talked to the clerk in the mercantile and was told the same thing. Old Doc Albert would know the directions to Kolvecks hunting lodge.

Toby climbed the steep steps with Pal right behind him. He knocked on the door. Then he knocked again and heard a voice say, "Come on in, the door is unlocked.

Toby tried to be friendly. He heard Doc say, "You can't bring that mutt in here. This is a doctor's office."

Toby opened the door and told Pal to, "wait" right outside of the closed door.

"What is it you want? Are you sick?" The doctor asked impatiently.

"No, no, I'm not sick. I came to ask if you could tell me where the Kolveck hunting lodge is. My father and Mr. Kolveck went hunting together," Toby said.

"No one's been there for years. Mr. Kolveck's son, Wilber, never wanted to hunt. His daughter always went hunting with him."

Doc Albert continued talking, "Wilber just wasn't normal. Something was wrong with him. I never could figure out what it was. He has spells like fits. The Kolvecks were just sick about him. Dora was the only one that could care for him."

Toby stood and listened then said, "Is the lodge far from here?"

"No," the doctor's hands pointed in every direction and Toby tried to keep up. Even so, he was sure he could find it.

Toby left while the doctor was still talking about Wilber.

↜ Chapter 45 ↝

Toby rode all day and into the night hours. Hoping he had interpreted the hand jesters of Doc Albert. Pal never tired. He ran next to Toby's horse when the path was wide enough. The horses zigzagged through the thick trees and thickets.

Toby was beginning to think he had gone in a wrong direction. He stopped his horse and crawled down to stretch.

The air felt heavy and then Toby realized what he could smell, it was smoke. He knew the lodge could not be far away. He decided to walk and lead the horses the rest of the way so no one in the lodge would see him coming.

The smoke smell was getting stronger so he tied the horses in an area he could get to in a hurry. Toby was as quiet as he could be. He instructed Pal to stay with the horses. He did not want him to scare up any birds and make a loud noise. Each step he took, he placed a foot down and then he would pause. It was so still and quiet except for the crush under each foot. He was determined not to let anyone in the lodge know he was coming. The lodge was hidden with years of overgrowth. He had no trouble approaching the front door.

Toby took a deep breath and knocked on the lodge door.

The latch clicked, and Toby was as close to the door as he could stand.

The door opened only a couple of inches. Toby's hand was on the door and pushed it open and walked in passed Dora taking her by complete surprise.

Toby said, "I'm so cold. Could I warm up by your fireplace?" He did not wait for an answer. He walked toward the fireplace. He acted as if he did not see the man setting on the old worn-out couch. He stood with his back to the man, rubbing his hands to get them warm.

Then Toby turned around and looked at the man.

"Henry, is that you?"

The man had been sitting with his head down. His hair hung down to his shoulders. Hair hung over his forehead and over his ears. His face was covered with whiskers.

Henry raised his head and starred.

"Toby, O Toby."

Then they all heard a click. It was a loud sound, and each one knew what the sound was. Their attention turned their heads to look toward Wilber holding a 12-gauge shot gun pointed at Toby.

With no hesitation Dora stepped over in front of the barrel of the shot gun. She grabbed the barrel of the gun , lowered it but holding it very tight.

"No Wilber, no."

⌒ Chapter 46 ⌒

Toby moved as fast as he could. He leaned down and helped Henry up on his feet. Toby put his arms around Henry and started him walking to the door. They reached the door.

Toby opened it and grabbed the buffalo coat and fur hat. Toby slipped the coat over Henry's shoulders while continuing to push him along. The two men slipped into the trees and out of sight of the lodge. Toby could hear Dora screaming at Wilber threatening him if he tried to stop the two men. Toby knew this was not the last time they would hear from Wilber.

Toby helped Henry up and onto the horse with the saddle and then said, "Hang on, Henry."

Toby rode the horse with only the saddle blanket on it. He took the reins and led the horse with Henry on it. They traveled most of the night and arrived at the cabin at dawn.

Chapter 47

Toby walked Henry to his cabin door and told him to knock.

Toby left him standing there and went to the bunkhouse.

Henry knocked one more time. The door opened and Rose stood looking at her beloved. Seven months of fear and doubt left her body. The weakness she felt engulfed her whole being.

"Rose, I'm home."

"Henry, is it really you?"

Henry had been leaning on the door frame. Suddenly his knees started to bend and he fell to his knees on the floor. Tears filled his eyes and rolled down onto his beard.

Rose lowered her body and was on her knees. Her body was tight against his. She put her arms around his neck.

With sobs she said, "I knew you would come back to me."

In a voice almost with no sound, she heard, "Rose, hold me."

Rose reached up and pushed his hair off of his face and looked into his tear filled eyes. She placed a hand on each side of his head and began to kiss him all over his face. She smothered his face in kisses.

Henry told her, "When I remembered you, I didn't think I'd ever see you or the twins again."

"Henry, you have a baby girl too. I have not named her. I have been waiting for you. You told me you had a name but would keep it a secret until she was born. Henry, she was born the day of the accident." Rose's voice ended in a crackling whisper.

"I remember, Rose. I do remember, Henry said.

"We have plenty of time." Rose whispered to him. Then she continued.

"Henry, it will take sometime for the twins to remember you but they will. I have talked about you every day to them."

In a very kind and considerate voice Rose said, "I would like to trim your hair and shave your beard before the children see you."

"Henry, you will need rest before you see the twins and your new daughter," she said. "We'll go down the hall to the last bedroom, and no one will know you're home and we can be alone.

✿ Chapter 48 ✿

Thomas had gone to the bunkhouse and heard the wonderful news. Rose found Thomas, Paul, Margaret and Inga holding Baby Girl outside of Henry's bedroom door waiting.

It brought tears to Rose's eyes. She cried so easily now.

The door slowly opened, and Henry stood looking thin, pallid and weak but he was alive and he was home.

Thomas jumped up and hugged his brother and had to be pried off. The little twins watched and did not move from their sitting position. Henry sat down on the floor next to his children. Rose sat down as close as she could to Henry. Touched his face and kissed him tenderly.

Then she said, "We have missed you so much. Haven't we, kids?"

Each little child moved a little closer. Henry talked softly to them so they would not be afraid of him. He reached his arms out to each one and they crawled up on his legs while he put his arms around them, then hugged and kissed each one.

Henry picked his twins up and walked down the hall to the kitchen where Rose and Inga had cooked a welcome-home dinner just for Henry and his family. The door of the cabin opened up, and all of the brothers walked in with all of the other hands who worked for Henry. Each greeted him with disbelief and tears in their eyes.

Henry sat down at the head of the table in his own chair where he always sat for his meals. He placed Margaret in the right high chair and Paul in his own chair.

Rose came into the kitchen carrying Baby Girl who was seven months old.

Rose handed Henry his baby girl.

Henry said, "Myra Eveline Donlin Higgins.

Rose spoke softly, "Oh Henry, it's a beautiful name."

The following days were spent celebrating Henry's return. Friends came to the cabin in surprise, shock and astonishment. It was now over seven months since Henry's terrible accident, and he was finally home. Rose had become very protective. Henry was getting stronger each day and wanted his old life back as if nothing had ever happened.

It was a time of placing a quilt on the grass in a perfect spot in the backyard. Sharing a picnic Inga had made. Rose and Henry watched as the twins played and Myra sat on the quilt by her father.

It was a time to watch Myra smile and giggle at her siblings. She was so content to sit on her father's lap. She cried to be carried everywhere by her father.

Rose tried not to hold Henry back but she sent a message privately to the bunkhouse. Everyone was to never let him go off alone. Thomas took it upon his own to be everywhere Henry was.

In the mornings Thomas arrived in the kitchen the minute Henry did and waited for Henry to eat his breakfast then follow him all day, every day.

❦ Chapter 49 ❧

It was two weeks since Henry returned home. The day started quiet and pleasant. The knock on the door sent Rose to answer it as she never let Henry go to the door alone in fear it would be someone she never wanted to see again.

Rose opened the door and looked into the eyes of Dora Kolveck.

The desperate shock showed clearly on Rose's face. She opened her mouth to speak.

Dora spoke in a whisper but Rose heard her clearly.

"I came to warn you." She paused and then said, "Wilber is missing. I do not know where he is. Please watch over your family and protect them."

Dora turned and left as quietly as she had come. She crawled up on the same wagon she and Wilber had taken Henry to the hunting lodge.

Rose quickly closed the cabin door and slipped the lock bolt in place. Then she made sure her family was all inside the cabin and safe.

Rose was clearly aware that all of her family and all of Henry's family needed to be told of Dora's visit and the warning she brought.

She sent Thomas to the bunkhouse in a hurry to tell all of Henry's brothers and all of the work hands to come to Henry's cabin immediately.

Inga was told to take all of the children to their room and no one was to go outside.

The situation could not be delayed. Rose needed to deal with it now. All of the men crowded into the kitchen and stood waiting to hear something that first, had to be important enough to call them into Henry and Rose's private home. Then each knew it had to do with each one here today.

Rose spoke first explaining every detail about Dora Kolveck's surprise visit. She tried not to scare anyone. As soon as she spoke they all realized just how scared Rose was, it was the sound of her voice. They had never seen her so nervous or heard her voice like this, even when she was searching for Henry.

Rose paused as if trying to remember something Dora had said. Then it came to her.

Dora had said, "Please help me find him. He is all I have."

∽ Chapter 50 ∾

Henry stood up slowly from his chair at the head of the table. He stood up straight with a determined look on his face and each one in the room turned to look at and listen to hear what Henry was going to say.

He said in a loud voice, "We must find him and we must find him now."

∽ Chapter 51 ∾

The knock was loud and penetrating. The person pounding on the door sounded desperate. Mr. Wiley Rineheart tried to get to his door before anyone on the street stopped and noticed. It was dark out and the man knocking could see a small light coming through the window.

As Wiley Rineheart's hand turned the door knob the man heard the click. His hands were on the door and he opened it nearly knocking Wiley Rineheart to the floor. He stepped in, turned and slammed the door closed.

Even with only a small amount of light in the room. Mr. Rineheart knew who he was looking at. They stood in the center of the room. Neither man spoke. Wiley Rineheart looked at the man's dirty clothes. His shirt and pants were torn. The boots he was wearing had mud clinging to the side and bottom of each boot.

He had not shaved for what looked like many days. He also looked as if he had not had a bath for many days.

Mr. Rineheart leaned down to the man and spoke slowly and clearly, "What in the ----- before he could finish the man grabbed his arm and said excitedly, "I need help, I need a place to hide." The man's voice was low and harsh.

Wiley Rineheart's face was pale and he stood frowning with his mouth open, staring intently at his cousin, Wilber Kolveck.

For additional copies of this or other
books written by Phyllis Collmann:
pac51@hickorytech.net
712-552-2375
www.collmannwarehouse.com

Baby Morrison

Twins Blake and Brenna